THE ILLUMINATED

ALEXANDER SEMENYUK

World Castle Publishing, LLC
Pensacola, Florida
Copyright © 2025 Alexander Semenyuk
Paperback ISBN: 9798891264403
eBook ISBN: 9798891264410
First Edition World Castle Publishing, LLC, September 15, 2025
http://www.worldcastlepublishing.com

Licensing Notes

Cover: Cover Designs by Karen
Editor: Karen Fuller

Dedicated to my dogs Pep and Jojo

FOREWORD

The desert wind harshly blew sand into my face as I struggled to see into the distance. I thought I saw movement, but I knew it was most likely my imagination, or perhaps a hallucination. With so much poison in the air, I could never be sure anymore.

One thing I was certain about was the dead man my dog Toko had found the other day. He was lying with his face in a puddle, after a rare day of rain. There was a large gash in his head, and the back of his shirt was ripped to ribbons. Evidently, he'd had company, though I wondered at my own assumption. After all, I hadn't had any company except for

Toko in five years.

I did not avert my eyes as the sand kept on coming my way. I was used to it, but also madly tired of it. At this point, I hated the dull color of the landscape, the scorching sun, and the monotony of mere survival. I no longer dreamed of anything better than just plain survival. Normal, real life was impossible on this planet now. Maybe in the future, someone would fix it before someone else destroyed it again, but not now.

One thing I did dream of was a change in scenery. I wanted to see green. Tall trees, rivers, and lakes.

I had put it off for so long, living here among the rocks in my wooden hut. Did I have the determination to actually make a change and move? Was my desire strong enough?

Perhaps the fact that I was running out of food and hadn't found an animal to hunt in weeks was another reality helping me to decide. Who was I kidding? Of course it was.

I called Toko over to me. The powerful, tall, slim dog lazily jogged towards me. I was always impressed with how long he had lasted. It seemed that he simply loved me too much to give up yet.

"Time to go home and rest."

The night was coming. Would I make that crucial decision, finally?

CHAPTER ONE
COLD REALITY

I sat at the same cracked old wooden table as I had every night for so many years. I had just one candle left. Simple and white, a lone survivor, like me. I carefully lit it and watched as the flame took. Toko lay down in the corner of the cabin; he looked exhausted. How would he travel? Especially on a leash, no way I could let him just wander around, with all the mutated creatures around…

I pulled out a grilled lizard and threw a piece to Toko. He caught it and began to gnaw on it. Even the dog was tired of this routine. I took a bite, and the taste was that of absolute monotony.

It was funny in a way, how all the stories of the past had described the human apocalypse. Films and books depicted hordes of zombies and deformed humans. Yet, it was the animals that actually grew strong and deformed, and we humans became weak and poisoned. Those who couldn't adapt to the poisoned air simply died, and that was the majority. The rest? Well, all I knew was that the beasts got most of the rest. Even the dead man I had found recently looked like a vulture or another large bird had attacked him.

I looked at Toko. "Tomorrow, we go towards the sea."

Toko raised his head. He understood one thing: I had said something new, and that was worth his attention.

He stared at me as I added, "We will

either get there, or we will die trying."

I placed an old, small, faded red compass on the table and then unfolded a map. I tapped the image of the water.

"To the east. Look at that…it's hundreds of miles."

A daunting journey. But should that bother me so much? Wasn't it all the same in the end? I believed that I'd go at the time meant for me, so why should I worry?

I lay on the wooden bench and watched the last light of the final candle fade. Then there was darkness.

CHAPTER TWO
THE CANYON

Our bodies could be trained like machines. Mine was no different. I woke up exactly when the first rays sneaked through the boards of my hut's walls, as I always did. Toko was slurping up water from his bowl. Once I sat up, he gave me a glance of acknowledgement. I began to pack.

Hunting knife — attached to my belt.

Revolver — also my belt.

Rifle — over my shoulder.

The rest?

Dried meat, matches, two metal bottles filled with water, tape, bandages, and one small bottle of precious peroxide all went into my backpack. The last thing was my family photo. I looked at it for a long time before putting it into the backpack as well.

Toko looked surprised and anxious, and his eyes were wary, as I put a leash around his neck. I tried attaching it to my belt, also making sure I had a handle on it whenever I needed to pull.

"You need it this time, buddy, trust me. Don't be mad."

Toko suddenly jumped up and scratched my cheek with his sharp claws. Instinctively, I smacked him on the side of the face. He instantly sank to the floor, and his eyes turned red. My anger faded at the sight of his frightened eyes and posture. I suddenly felt sad and ashamed.

I reached down and fondled his

ears. "Look, it's not easy for me either. I'm sorry, but you can't jump on me like that. We are going now." I pulled the leash, and he followed without further trouble.

It was a bright, sunny day, or rather scorching hot, with the air hanging heavily around me. The only way out of this desert valley was through a canyon, and that's the first place that made me nervous. I recalled elderly people, long dead, who had spoken about just how dangerous the trail through the canyon could be. But oddly enough, or maybe just annoyingly, I had forgotten exactly why.

As I made my way down a hill and entered the tall orange walls of the canyon, I knew that my pace, unfortunately, had to be slow. Good observation of my surroundings was key. If I neglected this aspect even for a few minutes, a predator could be upon me before I could pull out my firearm and react in any effective way.

I kept myself and Toko to the left wall, and we steadily progressed forward, or perhaps it was backward, and I just didn't know it, just like the rest of this civilization.

It was around noon that Toko began to cough a bit and dragged his feet. I took out a small bowl and poured just about a finger's worth of water. "Don't know when we'll find water again, so be strong, buddy." I patted him on the head.

Toko drank it instantly. I took my time and drank in tiny sips, really enjoying it. The dog looked at me longingly.

"Toko, why are you looking at me

like that with those big eyes? You could have taken your time, too."

We pressed on.

Around four, we heard the first sign of life besides ours, but I wished we hadn't. It was an ugly croak, preceded by a giant deformed condor landing upon one of the rock formations sticking out of the canyon wall. I stopped, pressed my back against the wall, and pulled out my revolver. I forced myself to breathe calmly and slowly, and relaxed in order to reduce the pace of my beating heart. The condor beast was watching us; his big red eyes bulged as he flew closer and landed on the ground, spreading his massive wings. I pointed the revolver right at his head. He stood there observing me, slightly moving his head from side to side. Toko let out a low growl. We were standing our ground. The condor could clearly sense that we weren't going to go down easily. He flapped his wings and flew out of the canyon.

I closed my eyes and took a deep cleansing breath. I was relieved that I hadn't had to use one of the six bullets in the revolver. We'd been able to meet the first challenge, but I was sure the condor would be watching us from now on. One slip-up and he would be on top of us. *Damn.*

At eight, the sun began to set, and Toko and I found a formation of large boulders that created almost a tent-like structure, with a slab sitting atop the others, creating a type of roof.

For some reason, the makeshift building gave me a sense of safety, which I knew was not the case at all. The most

I could hope for was some shelter from the elements, and perhaps any predator would make enough noise that I'd wake from what would surely be a light, fitful sleep. Still, I hoped for the best.

Things that make little sense often rule over us.

So I sat in the shelter of the rocky room and stretched out my tired legs. Toko lay down and placed his head on my thighs, looking at me with devotion in his eyes.

"That's great, buddy, don't give my sore legs any space to move." I smiled and scratched the dog under his chin.

I put my head on my backpack, which was leaning against the wall, and simply focused my eyes on a single spot on the wall of the canyon, dimly illuminated by the moonlight.

In the middle of the night, I woke up, shaking. It was *cold*. Toko barely opened one eye, obviously comfortable and not wanting to be bothered.

I guess the canyon's beasts did not like the cold either. None seemed to be around.

From that point on, I drifted in and out of sleep until the sun began to rise again. We both rose and stretched, and I continued to lead our two-man mission to nowhere, or to the sea. Whatever came first, anyway.

It was more of the same on the second day, however, once we got closer to the canyon exit, I noticed creatures I'd only heard about up high on the walls. I stared in fascination at the two-headed goats. They were great climbers. I remembered hearing about them and dismissing the story as a bad joke or a myth, yet here they were. Freakish. They let out disgustingly annoying sounds and somehow hopped from one tiny ledge to another. I could hardly believe what I saw as they simply defied logic, seeming to cling to the vertical surfaces.

Once they saw us, their harsh baaing became angry and more frequent. Their bright yellow eyes expanded, and their double heads swung back and forth.

I had read about freak circuses in some old books, and here I had a free ticket to the greatest one yet. I twitched Toko's lead to get him to hurry as I sped up my walking pace. The last thing I needed was these freak animals attracting more predatory birds. The canyon was almost at its end, but night was coming again, and I had no idea what we'd see up ahead, so I wanted to hurry and find shelter.

CHAPTER THREE
ECHOES OF THE FORGOTTEN WORLD

I don't know why I thought I would see greenery or tall trees. Interesting, how our experiences shape our expectations. I suppose some fairy tale had taken hold deep inside my mind. The landscape was still desert, now flat with sand and cracked, dry ground. Here and there were a few cacti. On the far horizon, however, there was a rectangular silhouette. I focused my gaze on it and increased my pace. Toko, however, was having a hard time keeping up.

"Can't stop here, we need cover," I whispered to him, gently tugging on the leash.

Poor dog. According to the map, we had at least two more days to travel in the desert until we reached a river. At that point, I was hoping that we would indeed see a significant change in our natural surroundings. My soul wanted to see green.

My throat was dry, causing me to cough. However, I didn't want to waste water.

I knew that most of the cacti here contained water that was toxic. Still, I managed to find one I could drink from. I crouched down, using my knife to carve out a deep hole in its trunk. Then I took a wooden straw I had made a while back and pushed it into the hole. I sucked on the straw and after a while, managed to suck out some drops. Without thinking, I moved my left hand forward to grasp the trunk of the plant and was stabbed with one of its spikes.

"Ahhh!"

Toko jumped, startled, and then licked my head. I curled my hand into a fist and finally got the liquid inside the cactus to drip from the straw. I caught some in a shallow bowl and gave it to Toko.

Pain and pleasure are like an inseparable brother and sister, forever holding hands.

Peering ahead at the shape in the distance, I said, "Let's keep going, Toko. I think I know what that is."

The silhouette drew closer, and I could tell that it was most likely an old trailer. I knew that many people used to live in them. I fervently hoped that there were no creatures living in this one now.

Soon we approached the building, and I was proven correct. I was an old trailer, painted white at some point, now looking yellow and rusty with the paint peeling off. I forced the door open, and heavy, stale air rolled out. I carefully stepped in and examined it. There were no creatures, but it was terribly hot inside, despite the shady interior. Toko seemed to be glad as he lay down at the foot of an ancient-looking couch. I left him there and began to look through the dusty drawers.

I found a piece of white paper with black faded words on it and some images. I guessed that it must be an old newspaper, though I had never seen one before.

What's the news now? I chuckled to myself. "A bunch of freaky, deformed beasts and birds have occupied the land. There are no humans left. Enjoy your week!"

How's that for news? I shook my head and set the paper aside.

I'd been taught that the most popular way of delivering news was on something called the television. I had seen a few of these devices when I was a kid, broken, of course, completely useless, but my memory of them was vague. There were other electronic items that were utterly useless now. I was told they were called "tablets" and "smartphones."

What was the point of "smart" technology if humans themselves had gotten so dumb as to cause all of this, their own end?

I looked at Toko, who, obviously exhausted, hadn't moved from his spot in front of the couch. His eyes were so tired.

I knelt down to pet him. He looked at me trustingly as I soothed, "But it's not the end yet, Toko, as long as I'm alive. There could be other people, too. We have to try and find out."

With a final pat on the dog's head, I heaved myself up and opened the last drawer. Finally, something useful! I lifted the bronze cup and peered at it in the fading light. Smiling, I said, "Now that is a beauty. When we get to the natural streams in the green forests, I'll drink from it." I placed it in my backpack. One can dream, after all, why not?

I sat on the couch right above Toko and waited for the night with my eyes half shut. From now on, I decided to move during the night and seek shelter during the day. At least until we got beyond the desert.

After a few hours' sleep, we got going again. At night, the desert's cracked earth was cool, and there was a slight breeze. Toko was moving slowly, and it irritated me, but at the same time, I couldn't be too upset with him. It had hit me as I sat on the couch in that old trailer that he probably was going to die before this journey was over, even if I survived. Then I'd be all alone for sure. All alone in the world. The big, wide world that had once been full of people. In older books, I had read about the concern about eventual overpopulation. Now the hysteria struck me as ironic. I couldn't find another human being even if I searched for days. Perhaps this was hell. I understood Toko's reluctance to keep moving.

Then, of course, the dog let out a low growl and stopped. The fur on his back stood up as he slowly turned his head back and stared at a deep fissure in the ground. Then I began to hear it too. The hissing. A thin, but abnormally long black snake with an elongated, narrow head and bright yellow eyes emerged from the crack.

A snake, venturing out in the cold dark?

"It doesn't get easier, does it?" I sighed and backed away, dragging Toko with me.

It crawled a bit further from us but kept its eyes on me the whole time. Then it stopped, as though it were frozen, just gazing into my face. Toko kept growling. I slightly pulled him.

"Let's go. We can't lose time."

The moment we began walking again, the snake started crawling, constantly keeping the same distance. It was odd–at night, and we were much too large to serve as prey. We weren't threatening it; what could be its motivation?

"Isn't this just a damn lovely stroll in the cool desert? A nice night, right, Toko?"

The dog looked up at me with huge eyes, giving me a "you idiot" look.

"Don't like my jokes anymore?" I stopped suddenly and turned toward the snake. "How about you?" I yelled at it, gesturing with my arm. The snake stopped.

"You cold-blooded, worthless creature without a soul, screw you. You'll never eat me."

We kept walking, and the snake kept crawling. This went on for the entire night.

As the sun began to rise, I was utterly exhausted. The snake found a new fissure to explore and slithered into the crack in the ground. Thanks a lot, you lousy reptile.

I sighed and scanned the distance, looking for daytime shelter. Not far off, I could see a large, broken highway bridge.

"Come on, hurry," I said to Toko, tugging on the leash. The poor dog's head was nearly on the ground as I pulled him.

"You'll sleep soon. I've seen this area on the maps. This used to be a major highway, which means we are doing well. Another night and we will see green and water! Maybe berries, leaves, some meat?"

Toko looked up when I said "meat".

"We still have some left. Let's get under that bridge, then you'll get food and water."

Before the rays fully illuminated my lonely world, we were in the shadow of the broken bridge, leaning against the grey concrete. I took off my boots and rubbed my sore feet. Fortunately, I hadn't developed any blisters. The cool concrete felt good on my bare soles.

I made good on my promise and gave Toko some water and some dried meat. He lay on one of the slabs, chewing it slowly. Finally, he'd learned that small pleasures were few and far between.

I tried to make myself comfortable, resting against my backpack. It was quiet under the broken bridge. Pieces of the old world...nothing more.

CHAPTER FOUR
THE CAVE

I was a little boy again, sitting on the porch. My dog, Karlo, sat by my side, intently looking out into the distance.

The screams were faint at first, but then they moved closer and closer. My father and uncle came out on the porch with rifles. My older brother and mother shoved a backpack into my hands. I saw Dad and Uncle now farther away from the house, setting themselves up behind large boulders.

"Dad says we must go into the cellar and then into the tunnel."

I turned to my brother, hardly believing my ears. "The tunnel that goes to those caves under the mountains? Isn't that scary?"

My brother's mouth was set in a determined line. "Dad says not as scary as what's coming."

"Then why isn't he coming!?"

"He's that kind of man. Don't run."

I stood and threw down the backpack. "This makes no sense! If he's not running, I won't either!"

My mother grabbed my arm and lifted me up. Karlo barked at her.

Her eyes were like flint. I knew that look brooked no arguments. "We go NOW!"

My mother seldom yelled at me, and this time I was frightened. As she pulled me into the house, I looked back at my father and uncle. They were holding the weapons and peering over the boulders. I allowed Mother to pull me into the house.

As the cellar cover closed, I heard the first shots. It was the last act of my father on this earth.

Mom kept dragging me into the tunnel, tears flowing down her face. My brother's face was twitching, but I knew he'd been preparing himself for this day. Dad had repeated to him for a year now: "You'll be the family leader soon, you must be strong."

Easier said than done.

The tunnel led to a small door. Beyond it was a series of ancient caves, which led out into a valley.

I woke up with Toko licking my face. It was getting dark. The dream still lingered, and I thought more of my childhood. I recalled all of the people I had seen killed by the beasts, including my brother. And I remembered all of the people I had seen die of terrible diseases, including my poor mother.

I gradually built immunity to the diseases and learned the patterns of the beasts. We had a community there in the desert canyons, and I traveled with them after my family was gone. But the others eventually died too. Even the younger people couldn't last. I learned that if your dreams were abandoned, and your goal was simply to survive another day, you had a better chance at doing just that.

But it seemed I had a dream now too: to see the water, and the green trees and grasses. I'd only read about those things, like the ocean.

I scratched Toko's ears and kissed his head, then I stood up. "You're all I have left now, boy, all I have left. Let's go; we must walk again. Let's go see that green." Toko willingly trotted alongside me.

The temperature had dropped, and the night was cooler than the previous few had been. Toko must have been more comfortable, as he was able to pick up his pace. I think I even saw a glimpse of a smile on that long and serious face of his.

From time to time, we'd hear a howl or a roar, but it all seemed very far away. The scenery was starting to change ever so slightly. There were more plants and hills, and up ahead were the mountains, which I knew were the key to making it to the next change in the terrain. A new landmark, if you will. According to my map, just beyond them were forests and rivers.

As the sun began to rise, we approached the foothills of the mountain range. I spied an opening that looked like a cave. I pulled Toko towards it, but he sniffed the air and resisted, planting his feet and refusing my tugs on the lead.

All I wanted was to sit in the darkness and rest. I said testily, "Come on, man! Like last time, we'll eat and rest, and then we'll see the green! We'll be able to drink fresh water! The sooner we rest, the sooner we can get up and go again, and get to the place where there will be water springs!" I pulled him harder, and he finally obeyed. Just as the sun began to heat up the rocks, we got into the shade of the cave. I did not go in very deep, simply situating ourselves far enough inside not to feel much heat.

I don't know why I so easily and

eagerly entered that cave, especially when my dog obviously knew it could be dangerous. I suppose I was just *so tired*.

Only a few hours had passed when I heard Toko's deep, low growl. Immediately, I awakened from my dozing. Toko's growl was an angry growl…one I knew too well. I opened my eyes wide and got a hold of his leash and my rifle. Up ahead, at the entrance to the cave, was the silhouette of an ugly, large, beastly, disgusting, deformed bear.

I slowly rose to my feet and began to pull Toko after me deeper into the cave. The bear was sniffing and adjusting, and then it moved towards us. I pulled Toko and ran; the dog ran right beside me. As the light disappeared, I had to adjust to the darkness and stayed close to the wall, feeling it, basically not knowing where we were going. I could hear the bear moving around in the cave, although it sounded far away.

We came out into an open area. Sun shone through a hole in the ceiling of the rocky room. There were a few tunnels leading off deeper into the mountainside, and when I hesitated, the bear emerged into the space and stood up on its back legs, roaring.

My rifle had explosive bullets, but looking at the size of the creature, I wasn't sure it would do much. I swiftly adjusted it from my shoulder and fired into the hideous beast's face. Blood flew from his head as he moved backward, and then he shook his head as if trying to get something out. I realized that the ceiling was shaking, and then it started to collapse. No more time to think. We ran into the closest tunnel as many rocks smashed down behind us.

I felt like we walked for hours in the dark, my legs moving almost of their own volition. I had never felt so tired in my life, but I was not about to stop and rest in an area I could not see.

But my reluctance to stop paid off when I heard a trickling sound. Then I felt water beneath my feet. I detached Toko's leash from my belt. The only choice was to go with the current, and it picked us up and moved us toward its exit. Bright light hit my eyes as we tumbled down a waterfall.

CHAPTER FIVE
THE GREEN

I felt a cool tongue on my face, licking my cheeks and forehead over and over again. I looked up. Toko slightly backed away, looking at me with big, worried eyes. I was happy to see him, but not just him. Right above me was…green. Green trees! I tried to sit up, but still felt numb and heavy. I slowly rolled over and then, with much effort, got on my knees and looked around. First, I spotted the waterfall we had fallen from, the pond at the base of the falls, and the stream that led away from the pond. I sat up on the sandy shore. Toko had pulled me out of the water and onto the shore. He was a miracle worker; he'd saved my life, not for the first time. I hugged him and kissed him on the side of the head. Then I saw my backpack and rifle. He had even gotten those to safety.

"Haha…you're amazing, buddy." Toko frolicked a bit, then shook water all over me.

I finally stood up and put the rifle on my left shoulder and the backpack on my right. Then I re-attached Toko's leash to my belt.

I had to stand for a few minutes and just admire the green. It was a feast for my eyes. How many years since I'd seen green like this? Too many…And Toko? He must have been a very young puppy the last time he'd experienced streams like this one or trees like this.

Streams…I turned towards the

water, fell on my knees, and drank like a dog myself. Then I remembered the bronze cup. Ceremoniously, I drew it from my backpack, filled it from the stream, and gestured toward the trees in a toast. "To the green!"

I drank the cup dry, then I refilled the bottles.

I saw a flash of silver in the stream."It's a fish!" Wonderingly, I watched it swim away. A fish! I'd only seen pictures of fish in books before. I wondered if it was safe to eat. I addressed Toko. "I don't know why I always ask if something's safe to eat. Nothing in the world is safe to eat anymore, but we have to eat something to survive. Maybe we should catch one and cook it."

But before I did that, I took out some of our last portions of dried meat and handed them to Toko. "You deserve it more than I do, buddy."

The dog ate it with pleasure, and I smiled, watching him.

"I'll hunt once we find a place to camp here for a while. I hope we can. At least for a bit." I breathed the fresh, damp air and stretched my arms out above my head. "Let's spend some time among these trees and forests, then go to the big water…the ocean."

I stood up and we began our venture into the dense, beautiful, green trees.

I was fascinated by how tall they were, reaching up towards the sky. I felt like a child with a delightful new plaything. Every minute, I tried to refocus as I realized I was opening myself up to danger, but I just couldn't help it. The green! It was so good for my eyes, my soul…

"Toko, isn't this amazing…why couldn't people just be happy with this? Ah, look at this!"

I had spied some bumpy red berries growing on bushes. They were plump and luscious-looking. Without thinking, I plucked one off the bush and popped it into my mouth.

A mix of sour and sweet woke my taste buds. A smile grew on my face. I didn't think I'd ever tasted anything like this. I tried to remember the name I'd read in one of the old books. Toko sniffed at the bush and carefully pulled one off to eat.

"Aha! I remember! Raspberries! That's what they are!"

Toko gave a little yip and seemed to

smile as well. In a short time, we cleared the whole bush.

"Now that's a boost!"

There was still plenty of daylight left as we continued our exploration. There were mushrooms, roots, and moss–things I'd read about and viewed pictures of, but I could not remember if I'd ever seen them for real.

I pressed my finger into the green moss by a large, thick tree. It was damp, soft, and slightly moist. "Toko! It rained here recently! This is so much better already, do you see Toko? We barely survived, but this is good."

We wandered the forest for hours. I spotted a few small birds, which did not look dangerous or malformed, but they were too small for me to hunt with my rifle. I would need to set some snares.

I no longer felt tired, and I lost track of time. Once the sun began to set, however, I hurriedly began looking for shelter. Then a new blessing came our way as we stumbled into a small clearing surrounded by the trees. In the center was a wooden cabin.

"Well, what do you know…a miracle."

Miracle or not, I had my revolver ready. Even if there were people still alive here, it didn't mean that they'd be glad to share.

Cautiously, I approached the door. I knocked on it. "Anybody here?" There was no answer, so I pushed on the door and it creaked open.

As I went inside, it became very apparent that the owner no longer lived there. It smelled musty, and there was a light coating of dust on everything. The occupant must have died…or left recently.

I found some candles in one drawer, and matches, and to my great joy, a large wooden container of salt in another. There was also a small fireplace with a black iron pot in it. There was one wooden chair. No bed, no table. One window without glass, but covered with netting. That was it, but it was also plenty– so much more than I ever expected.

As night came, Toko and I finished the last of our food. Sitting by the candlelight, I was keen to hunt, but first I needed sleep. It was a shame to put out the beautiful flame of the precious candle. I sat marveling at it for at least an hour. In the dark, I lay next to Toko on the wooden floor and drifted away.

The sound of rain woke me up, but it was more than welcome. The smell after the rain was my favorite. Toko and I sat by the window watching as it fell upon the trees, grass, and bushes. Then came that wonderful scent.

We went outside, and the first thing I did was touch the wet grass with my hand and run my fingers through it. I held up my hand, and the drops spread down my arm, spreading like little rivers. It was the simple joys of life like this that still made it worth it somehow. Perhaps that was the essence of why I still kept on going.

I turned to my canine companion. "Time to hunt, but this time you'll stay here."

I can't say I saw much disappointment in Toko's face as I tied his leash to the cabinet inside the cabin, closed the door tightly, and set out with my rifle. The reason for this was simple. I didn't know what kind of beasts were here, and it was too dangerous to expose Toko in such a way. All I had to do was find the right spot and be patient.

Not much time had passed before I found another bush of raspberries. I situated myself in a thick shrub near a tree right across from the berry bush, and with my rifle ready, I began the waiting game.

It was not until I heard a strange, prolonged sound that I realized that I had dozed off. Startled, I looked through the opening in the shrub. Above the berry bush stood a very tall beast with antlers. It had two heads branching off a long neck. I recalled a similar animal called a deer from one of my picture books, but this one? Not really. But I took aim and fired. The beast shook, letting out a loud scream, and then collapsed.

Was it even safe to eat that thing?

Well…I'd just go back to my life philosophy. Do or die.

I took out my knife, and after a lengthy and utterly untidy dress-out, I had some meat in a bag to take "home." I was glad that salt was there, too!

I built a fire and cooked the meat in the black iron pot. The delicious scent filled the room, and Toko stood right next to me, watching my every move, with big eyes and his tongue hanging out. From time to time, he gave me a nervous glance.

Laughing, I assured him, "Yes, this meat smells good. Don't you worry, you'll get a share."

I scratched behind his ear and laughed again. The poor dog was very worried about getting the meat, and he was extremely happy when it was finally between his teeth. I sat in the wooden chair and slowly enjoyed some meat myself. I had no complaints; this was a great fortune. A small home, beasts to hunt, and berries.

"Maybe, Toko, we should stick around here longer than we planned, enjoy this opportunity, and move on at the right time."

What was the right time? I never knew.

I could imagine every thinking human had pondered and asked questions about the right time for whatever they needed or planned.

How many humans had asked this question before the destruction of the world had come? What great plans had they dreamed of?

None of those plans mattered when the cities were crushed and blown to ash. None of those plans mattered when the beasts took over the lands. None mattered when the air became poisoned.

Toko and I were survivors, and that was a miracle.

Thinking of air now, I did realize that it felt fresher here in the forest.

"Hmmn, Toko, maybe it's even better by the big waters. The ocean. Can you imagine the waves…the wind? I wonder how it feels?"

Did humans always want a little more? And is that what led to their destroying everything?

Once again, I watched the same candle, about halfway burned away now. Then I put it out and lay next to Toko on the flat wooden floor to have my rest. The dog was already snoring, with his legs stretched out. He had eaten well, and it was quiet. For him, that made it a very good day.

Toko did not worry about tomorrow. He just took what was in front of him, living in the moment.

That was just one of the big differences between us. Some days, I wished I were more like him, content to eat, sleep, and be alive. Other days, I loved thinking about what lay in the future and conjuring fantasies of what lay ahead.

Perhaps my end was near, and I had no clue. I snorted. Somehow, there

was beauty in that.
        I drifted away into the darkness.

CHAPTER SIX
NOT ALONE

The forest was vast and beautiful. For days, Toko and I simply spent time exploring nearby areas. I caught fish in the stream where Toko had saved me, made rabbit stew, and found a small lake, which quickly became my favorite spot. Toko and I would sit there, simply enjoying the stillness and the lovely scene, for hours. I watched the calmness of the lake, a breeze gently rippling the water from time to time, and listened to the natural world around me. I loved watching the leaves float by, like my thoughts.

There was one thing that I still

longed for despite finding this peace. I
craved human contact, a word, just to
know that I was not alone in this world.
That I wasn't the last one.

Those prayers were soon to be
answered.

Weeks passed as we contentedly
lived in the tiny house in the woods. Then
one of the days when I was out hunting,
I came onto an unfamiliar hill. From it, I
saw a tall structure among the trees that
I had never seen before. I figured it must
have been an old observation tower. My
theory was confirmed as I got closer to the
building. There was a tall ladder attached
to it, leading all the way up. Filled with
curiosity and excitement, I began to climb,
but not without caution, as I tested each
rung before going up further. By the time
I got to the top, I felt pretty winded, yet

the view was absolutely worth it. I was above all of the trees, seeing around me for miles and miles. With a smile on my face, I began to observe each direction with great patience and attention to detail.

I hadn't seen many birds in the forest until now. Large birds were soaring above the trees further ahead, closer to the mountains. Looking back, towards where we had come from, I could see the parts of the desert through the openings of those mountains.

On the right side, past the cabin, I noticed a structure that seemed to be built from grey stones. It was difficult to make out precisely what it was, not that I'd know for sure either way, but now I was more curious about that than anything.

However, the day was ending, and

after carefully climbing down the ladder, I went to the cabin to feed Toko and rest. Sleep did not come easily as I couldn't stop wondering about the stone structure and imagining all kinds of things that might be in it. Eventually, in the middle of the quiet night that was only broken by Toko's occasional snores, I finally fell asleep.

I woke up with the chirping of a bird, which was the first I'd heard here, or in many years, actually. I took this as a good sign, perhaps a forecast of positive things coming our way.

I heated up some water in the iron pot and poured it on top of herbs I'd gathered from the forest. One of the things the last elder had taught me before he died was how to make tea. He had an old book with various information on herbs and told me I should study it. After he was gone, I had plenty of time on my own to read, so I re-read that book multiple times. Today I was especially grateful to that man, as I sipped on my tea, enjoying its taste and aroma.

Toko curiously observed me.

"You can't have this, you'd have a stomach ache. Well, actually, I don't know, but I won't risk it. Relax, lie down, I'm going alone today again. There's something I have to see. I am going to check out an old building. You never know what we can find in the ruins of the old world." I paused, scratching Toko's scruff at the back of his neck. "Heh…a treasure? A treat or meat for you, maybe?"

Toko's ears went up for a moment at the mention of meat and treat.

Shaking my head, I chuckled. "Ha...that's what's on your mind. Every day, right? I can't blame you, but I want something more." I looked into Toko's eyes, and he stared back, trying to comprehend. "Something I can't even explain. Surviving, merely just surviving, is not enough for me. I want to really live...to connect, to see the world begin to heal." Toko rolled over, begging me to scratch his tummy. I complied, continuing my monologue. "I want to see people in the world rebuilding. I want to see families, laughter, children... See people in it. People who are not sick from poison in the air, or being hunted by beasts." I shook my head again, staring into Toko's eyes. " Is that too much to ask? Is it too crazy of a dream?"

Toko rolled over and stood,

stretching back, and tilted his head, watching me. He was trying to understand, poor thing.

As I stood up, I said, "Maybe it's a good thing you don't understand, but you still feel my energy, and you understand on a certain level."

I hugged him and then tied his leash.

"You continue to guard this place for us, and I'll be back soon."

I swung the rifle over my shoulder, kissed Toko on his hard forehead, and walked out the door to be greeted by the radiant rays of the rising sun.

"Ok, which way do I need to go?" I mused. I checked my compass to be certain and then began my walk toward the structure I had seen from the tower.

It was like being a child, seeing

something for the first time, and making new discoveries. That was how I felt, heading towards that building.

After some time, I thought I must have taken the wrong way. I thought I should have reached the stone building long before I got there, but suddenly, there it was.

It was a rectangular structure with a tower that was partially broken at the top. The building was constructed of grey stones and dark wood. On the side, I saw an old sign, but half of it was broken off and lost.

"Church of…"

A church! A place of faith. I stopped for a minute. It had been a very long time since I had seen one. Not since my father died, but my mother and brother prayed every night.

I still prayed, after a fashion…just in my mind, in the depths of it. I wasn't sure why I prayed, or whether some eternal Being existed, or listened to me. Perhaps my prayers, my longings, were simply to see the ocean or to meet other people again.

I pushed the old, heavy black door open. My senses were instantly alerted as I saw movement in the back of the church, illuminated by the rays coming in from the broken roof and windows. I immediately raised my rifle, my heart pounding. But then I saw them, and slowly lowered the weapon.

My eyes filled with tears. They were sitting against the wall, watching me with fear in their eyes. A woman and a young girl.

I slung my rifle over my shoulder

and held up my hands, then I sat a few meters away from them.

"You…you are real?" I asked, my voice shaking.

They both nodded.

Tears filled my own eyes, and my voice broke. "Please, forgive me. It's been so long, just so long. I was starting to think…that it was just me."

The woman nodded and spoke. "We haven't seen another…normal human in a very long time, either. I am Stella, and this is my daughter May. She does not speak; her vocal cords were damaged by the air."

I noticed some small purple bumps on their necks. They had the tell-tale signs of the disease but probably did not know it, and I wasn't about to alarm them.

Something else was far more

concerning. "You said normal, is there another kind?"

Stella nodded. "There was one we saw…we are not sure if it was human once, but we found shelter here, and we have survived for a long time."

I brightened a little. "Yes, this forest seems to be better than some other places!

"I have a dog with me, he is at a cabin I found. Do you want to go there before it's dark? It'll be safe to talk there some more."

Stella nodded, and she and May stood and followed me out of the church into the sunshine.

CHAPTER SEVEN
THE CANDLE AND THE SHADOWS OF LIFE

At first, Toko did not know how to react. He was confused and alarmed by the strangers, but at the same time, he was curious about the girl, May, who was kind to him, constantly petting him and giving him scratches. After several days, he looked proud of himself each time she smiled at him. It was strange for me as well, and for a while, I had trouble finding the right words. One-sided conversations with a dog for five years will do that. However, I, too, was doing better after a few days.

On the fourth day, I was able to get another rabbit. Mixed with some herbs and mushrooms, I made a savory-smelling stew for everyone. It was dark by the time I served two cups to Stella and May, a bowl for Toko, and as for me, I just got some of the meat I had dried and lit two candles. I insisted that Stella sit on the chair. I sat against the wall on the floor, not far from her, and May was comfortable cuddling with Toko.

I watched Stella first observe her daughter with loving eyes, then she looked out the window. I doubted she could see much. The candlelight illuminated one side of her face. I found her very pretty, and I wanted to know more about her, but at the same time, knowing that she and her daughter didn't have much time left to live, did I want to get close? I had waited for human contact for so long, but now it made my heart ache for them…

or perhaps for myself. They'd go on to a better place, I thought. Well, I hoped. I decided to learn more.

Casually, and in a friendly way, I asked, "So, where were you born, Stella?"

She slowly turned her head to me. "It used to be known as Florida, the state."

Excitedly, I asked, "By the sea, or the ocean, I mean?!"

She smiled in a tired way. "Yes, but I don't remember much anymore. We escaped by going north, and then, we went further and further inland."

"Did you find a community?" I put a log on the cooking fire, and the flames illuminated her face a little more.

"Yes," she nodded, "not far from here. There were twenty of us then, but now I have even forgotten some of their names."

"Did you have many books?"

For a moment, Stella looked surprised at this unusual question. "No, just a few kids' books. We knew nothing of what was happening. Did you know much?"

I leaned back against the wall. "At one point, a scientist who was studying the air and the early birth defects, the deformities, joined us. He said that after the final acts of war, there were almost no functional facilities left, and he couldn't continue any research, but he told us what he knew. I don't remember most of it, though. Doubt it would do me good either way."

She gave a short laugh, without mirth. "You're right. What can do us any good?"

We were silent for a few minutes. Then I continued, "Hmm, so, um, you and your daughter are the last ones? How hard has it been to survive?"

"Yes, the last ones here. I honestly am not sure how we even managed this long. It's a miracle." But the look on her face gave the lie to her words. Nothing miraculous about the tremendous effort in trying to survive alone.

I lightened the mood a bit. "Maybe it was her destiny to meet Toko."

We both laughed, and hearing human laughter again brought great joy to my heart. Then Stella asked me, "How long do you plan to stay here?"

"Not too long. I want to see the ocean."

She hesitated, then asked, "Will you take us with you?"

The question brought more sadness as I forced a smile. "Of course, if you want to go."

The woman's eyes suddenly took on a fire, and I saw what she must have looked like before she became so exhausted and careworn. "We are so tired, exhausted. Sitting here, I finally realized just how tired I am. It feels like every part of my body is in pain."

The candle was low and flickered. May was asleep with Toko on the floor. As I lay down, Stella lay next to me and quietly placed her head on my chest.

"Your heart is beating so fast…are you worried?"

Looking up at the dark ceiling, I wanted to say yes, that I was terrified and heartbroken. What I whispered to her, however, was also true. "Just happy, very happy you are here. It's so good to have human touch again."

She kissed my cheek and fell asleep with her head on my shoulder. I did not move all night, nor did I sleep. I wanted to take every single moment of that feeling into my soul. And I did.

Then the morning came.

As we continued to live together, Stella remarked that the days and nights went slowly, and she was grateful for it.

For me, however, the days moved fast, as I constantly wondered when the disease would take them.

Another week passed, and they both developed a heavy, dry cough, and their necks and backs began to constantly itch. These were symptoms all too familiar to me, as I remembered so many of my older companions in the desert coming to their end after this.

Stella was a fast-burning candle in my life. She had illuminated this moment in my journey, but consequently, the shadows became darker and darker.

The only thing I could do was comfort her with kindness and love. I held her every night and always made her tea.

May died first. She simply did not wake up one morning, lying next to Toko. Her face was illuminated by the sun's morning rays, and she looked peaceful. Toko kept licking her face and pushing her head with his nose, then he lay down next to her and cried together with Stella.

The grief and the pain from the loss took away any last strength that Stella possessed. She died the very next day.

I had no shovel, so I labored hard

after making a sharp tool out of wood, sort of like a spear. I buried them together, deep in the ground by the cabin. With my knife, I made an inscription on a plank and on the cabin door.

"Stella and May lived and died here."

CHAPTER EIGHT
ABNORMALITY

There are moments in life, like this one, when grief and sadness are so powerful that one has the overwhelming feeling of giving up, throwing up one's hands, and lying down to die among the grass and trees. This was how I felt after Stella and May died.

Then, I would see Toko standing there, wagging his tail, and he would lick my face, put his paw on my leg, and do everything he could to cheer me up. This gave me a push and some extra strength to get out of the dark feeling and keep going.

I decided to venture beyond the

ruined church and see what else I could find. One fine morning, I traveled again to the place where I had found Stella and May. But what I found next was truly horrifying.

Among the trees, I found a sort of trail. There were broken branches and bushes, small bones along the way, and spots of dried blood. At first, I figured this to have come from a deformed wolf, but as I moved along this trail, there was a terrible stench that got stronger and stronger. I cautiously crept through some undergrowth as the smell grew nearly unbearable. I peered through the bushes and saw a clearing.

In the middle of the clearing, among a large pile of bones and rotten meat, sat a pale-looking creature. It had a body structure that was similar to a human, but it was completely hunched and twisted. Its head was large and bald, its fingers were very long with sharp nails, and when it turned its face, the mouth gnawing on a meaty bone, chills crawled down my spine, and I nearly gasped aloud.

It had a giant mouth filled with long, sharp teeth, above were two deep, dark nostrils, and the eyes were thin, long, and completely red. In the horrific pile of bones, I could see human skulls. This monster did not discriminate.

I slowly began to back up, and at that moment, the creature dropped the bone and looked like it was either trying to listen or to catch a scent, which I imagined was hard with all of the rotting detritus around it. However, a bit terrified, I stopped moving. The creature went on eating.

For hours, I was stuck there until the rain came to my rescue, and the monster curled up and went to sleep. Just before dark, I was able to make my escape and get back to Toko in the cabin, but the thought of that monster finding us in the night terrified me. I began to think about leaving almost immediately. I calmed myself down a bit, reasoning that, fortunately, the thing had never come here. Not yet, at least. However, I knew it would eventually, sooner or later.

That very night, I started planning for our departure, perhaps in another week.

I watched one of the last remaining candles as long as I could this time, until it got all the way to the end, and then all that was left of it was the scorched black wick in the thin air, which fell into ash. Plunged into darkness, which I had dealt with easily before, I couldn't get my mind off that abnormal creature. Had it once been human? I felt it must have been.

I took a mental inventory of my ammunition. I only had five of the six bullets in my revolver, and only three rounds for the rifle. I hoped it was enough.

Perhaps the monster was something I could have become. Some bodies reacted differently to the poisons. Most simply died quickly. Many developed a disease over time and eventually succumbed to it. Once their immunity became compromised, like Stella and May. But it was possible that, over time, the viruses or bacteria or poisons caused changes in the body itself.

I had no idea what my side effect was, or if I ever would experience one. Maybe it had yet to manifest. I sincerely hoped I would not end up like that creature.

I gazed through the window at the grass and trees outside, gently illuminated by the moonlight. I could hear Toko snoring. Since May had died, the dog had whimpered and cried every evening before falling asleep, but tonight, he hadn't. Perhaps he was beginning to heal.

My eyes began to get heavy, and my head began to droop. Blinking, I began to rise in order to get ready for sleep. But I noticed motion outside the window and immediately felt adrenaline rush through my body, making me wide awake and alert.

It slowly crawled out of the bushes. The monster's narrow red eyes seemed to fix upon me. It was thirsting for my blood; I could see it licking its lips. It began to crawl towards the cabin.

My breath came in quick, shallow puffs. I knew my rifle was just there against the wall, yet I was frozen. I could do nothing as it opened the door and peeked in at me. Then it crawled and crouched over Toko, opening its large mouth…I could do nothing!

I startled awake. There was a cold sweat on my forehead and drops of sweat on the windowsill. My heart pounding, I quickly checked on Toko. He was sleeping soundly. I held my hand over his rising chest.

"You're all I have, buddy…"

I stretched and prepared to lie down next to him, but I heard a rustling in the bushes outside. Again, my body tensed, washed with adrenaline, and I carefully approached the window and looked out.

My hands began to shake as I saw two long pale arms and a large head with red eyes emerge from the shrubbery. It was sniffing the air. Horrified, I realized that I must have given it a new scent to follow when I tracked it earlier. But unlike in my dream, I grabbed my rifle and pressed myself against the wall with it aimed at the door. I worked on calming my wildly beating heart, which was trying to break through my chest, and steadying my breathing. Breathe in, breathe out. I swallowed hard.

Do or die…

Simply do or die.

Kill it or die.

Finally, I heard it moving around the cabin. Several times it scratched the walls and then the door. As its ugly head and horrible eyes appeared in the window, peeking in, I sank further into the shadows. I could hear and see its strange deep nostrils moving and sucking in air. Thankfully, Toko had stopped snoring and did not wake up.

After a few minutes like this, the creature moved away, and I strained to hear its progress as it crawled back into the forest. Only then did I start to move my own tense body.

I lowered my rifle and realized that my shirt was soaked with sweat, and my hands were shaking like the leaves in the wind. Out of all the terrible situations I'd faced, for some reason, this thing terrified me the most.

When the morning came, I realized that I had fallen asleep sitting against the wall, when Toko licked my face to wake me up.

We had to leave immediately, so I started stuffing the backpack.

CHAPTER EIGHT
THE CHASE

Years ago, when everyone in our desert settlement was still alive, I craved being alone and away from people. I'd often go and sit on my own up in the mountains and watch the desert.

But not anymore. Even leaving the graves of Stella and May was hard. They had been my first human company in over five years. Even if it was only a very brief moment in time, having them meant a lot to me.

With Toko on his leash by my side, I said my final farewell to them. I examined the map once more before heading out. Unfortunately, we had to travel near where the humanlike creature lived. I hoped it would be just far enough away from its lair that our scent would not carry to it.

I could not have been more wrong.

Toko noticed it first, growling. Then I saw it, moving through the trees, just outside our clearing. It watched us with its red eyes, but it did not attack.

My heart sank. I knew we could not return to the cabin and barricade ourselves in there. Pushing down my fear, I tugged on Toko's leash and hurried along.

I picked up the pace, and so did the creature, keeping the same distance and watching. Perhaps that was why it was a successful predator. It took a cautious approach, exhausting its prey, then pouncing at the right moment.

I focused on getting to a wide river before nightfall. Intuitively, I knew that was my only hope. As long as the monster did not change its strategy, I figured once we got there, we'd have more options for escape.

It was about a mile into this strange and terrifying chase that I lost sight of the creature. I slowed my pace a bit and noticed how hard my heart was beating, and my breathing was irregular. Fear hung on me like a wet blanket.

I stopped and stood by a large tree and drank some water. As I returned the water into the backpack, Toko growled, looking back.

"Oh no…"

I looked back and saw the narrow red eyes staring at me through the undergrowth. It was now directly behind us and closer. This made things more complicated. I obviously couldn't keep an eye on it as I moved forward, so I took my rifle and aimed at the monster, but hesitated. What if my bullets didn't hurt it? I only had three. It would know I had no defenses. But the moment I took aim, the creature quickly crawled behind a nearby tree.

I lowered the rifle, cautiously relieved. "Oh…it knows."

I surmised that when it was human, it must have killed men with weapons. Either that, or it had been shot and hurt. Too bad someone else's aim hadn't been so good.

I swung the rifle over my shoulder again and started walking. Toko's ruff stood on end, and he continually looked back at the creature, baring his teeth.

Each time he growled, I turned around and took aim with the rifle, and every single time, I saw it dive behind a large rock or a tree.

This constant, strange dance tired me quickly. Our progress was slow, and by midday, I was sure that we were still very far from that river, and I wondered if I could keep it up after nightfall. If not, we were surely going to die.

I began to jog despite the pain in my feet from blisters on my heel and toes. I had to continue to repeat the turning around trick, but now at least we were running. No matter how tiring or hard this was, our lives depended on it.

The afternoon wore on, but I was quickly losing steam. I could no longer run. I still turned and aimed my gun at the monster, but I could tell it knew

I was reaching the point of complete exhaustion. The look on its horrible face had changed from fear to an evil satisfaction. It still hid from my firearm, but it seemed to know I wouldn't use it.

Yet, the powerful sound of running water rejuvenated my spirit, and I summoned up a new burst of energy. We ran towards the sound and came upon a large, wide river. On the left side were the stony remains of an old collapsed bridge, and it looked good enough for us to cross, but not without getting wet. Not a problem!

Without looking back at the creature, I leaped onto the remains of the bridge and carefully hopped from one stone to another. Toko just swam in the water.

About halfway, I pulled Toko onto

a large stone in the middle of the river and looked back. I could see the creature peering out of the undergrowth, not too close to the water. It was clearly afraid of the river. Just for a last show of confidence, I aimed my rifle at the monster. It turned and ran away into the forest.

Gotcha. I thwarted your plan, you disgusting mutant!

"We did it, Toko…"

I began to laugh hysterically, as relief flooded my body. Despite the exhaustion and having the odds stacked against us, we had survived once again.

Do or die.

That's all there was to it. And we just kept doing.

Once we made our way to the opposite riverbank, I sat against a tree trunk and deeply exhaled. Night was coming. In the back of my mind, I wasn't sure it was safe to fall asleep there, but I was too exhausted to resist.

CHAPTER NINE
ONCE IT WAS A FARM

The days turned into weeks and weeks into months. This part of the journey seemed monotonous, but I was so grateful. We did not encounter any more threats from the beasts, and we were able to find berries and snare rabbits and birds to eat. Though it was good to have a break from surviving against the beasts, I could never really let my guard entirely down. Still, the days flowed into a good rhythm, and we were able to continue our journey in relative safety. Toko was by my side, as usual, being my trusted companion no matter what.

The leaves on the trees began to

change, and the world around us was no longer green, but a mix of glorious colors–red, yellow, orange, and the occasional evergreen. It was like magic. The leaves triggered a memory from my childhood of autumns long past. I picked up a few fallen leaves and showed them to Toko.

"This is autumn, or fall. The trees lose their leaves and go dormant for the winter. Then spring comes, and they get new leaves."

But occasionally a bit of despair crept into my more buoyant mood, and I let the leaves drop to my feet. "What is the point of titles, labels, and names now? I'm not sure. We are just living."

Indeed. We were just living, nothing less and nothing more. All things that were at one point considered important no longer meant anything.

I pondered as I trudged along with Toko. Were those things ever important in the first place, if an event can render them useless? What makes something truly important?

We came upon a small, clear lake, and I sat down at the water's edge, next to Toko. The colorful leaves floated gently upon the water.

There were feelings I had left behind, along with all my relationships. I had almost forgotten love. A tiny spark of it still lingered in my heart, and I thought of my family and wondered if there was a life hereafter when I would see them again. Love…it was the one thing that could reach throughout the universe, perhaps forever. That's what truly mattered.

As those autumn leaves fell from

the trees and brought peace and calmness to me, so did my remembrance of my family, and the love I felt for my faithful companion, Toko.

I hugged my devoted dog and gave him a kiss on the forehead. His face remained serious, but I saw his tail wag.

"You're all I have now…in this whole world. Imagine that. Even if I thought up many different futures as a kid, I never thought this would become my reality. It never even made the list." I buried my hand in Toko's thick fur.

We continued our journey through fields and forests. As the fall drew near its close, we came upon a field with a white wooden house surrounded by a long porch. On one side stood a tall white barn. Paddocks and corrals were delineated by white wooden fences, but the fences were broken in many places.

"This is what used to be called a farm, Toko."

As I said this, we suddenly heard a loud howl. Other animals joined in. Just beyond the farm property was a hill, and a group of wolves sat there, noses pointed to the sky, howling. Though they were far away, I knew they must have caught our scent.

Toko and I ran to the farmhouse and forced the old front door open, then shut it behind us. I looked around and saw an old wooden table. I pushed it against the door, hoping that would be enough. I hurried to the next room, which had a broken window facing the hill where the wolves had gathered. I readied my rifle, knowing that I did not have enough ammunition to take out all the wolves.

The wolves were trotting swiftly towards the house. I pointed the rifle through the broken glass.

There were six white wolves, but in the middle ran a large black wolf, whom I assumed was the alpha male. As he turned his monstrous head towards the farmhouse, his red eyes reminded me of the humanoid creature that had followed us so many months ago.

The wolves surrounded the farmhouse, baying at the sky. Toko was growling and shaking. I had no time to think; action had to be taken. I fired at the closest white wolf. He let out an agonizing sound as the bullet hit his neck and exploded. He fell to the ground, bleeding out.

The rest of the pack surrounded

him, and as he died, they all turned their heads towards the window. The black wolf came forward and watched me with those red eyes. As I aimed at his head, he leaped sideways to the side, and with a howl, he led them away back up the hill, and presumably into the nearby forest.

I exhaled and put the rifle down. I slid down the wall and scratched Toko's neck. He was still shaking.

"It's okay, buddy, tonight we can have some wolf meat. Your revenge, right?"

Toko looked like he was smiling, his tongue lolling.

"That's right, boy! Haha."

We explored the farmhouse. One important thing I noted right away was the large fireplace. As I searched, I didn't find many remnants of the previous inhabitants. There was an old, stained mattress that made the floor look comfortable. No bedding was left. I guessed critters had made nests of any clothing, if any of that still remained. There were no shoes or boots, and only a couple of threadbare towels in what must have been a linen press. I did find an old black jacket inside a closet, but it was too small for me. In the kitchen, there were some shards of broken dishes, and one small bronze pot, and an iron skillet. They were dirty, but usable. I held up the pot and showed it to Toko.

"You see? Wolf stew."

I cautiously went outside, and while I dressed out some meat, I left Toko tied to the porch, so he could alarm me if the wolves came back.

That night, I got the fireplace going

with some twigs and broken pieces of wood from some of the furniture. Then I placed the pot with water, salt, and wolf meat in the embers. It wasn't going to be anything too tasty, but food was food, and we needed to survive. Toko seemed to enjoy the scent regardless, and he ate his share of the meat with gusto.

The next step was boarding up the broken window. I found a few nails and some boards in the barn, and unbelievably, several boxes of ammunition for my rifle and a few extra rounds for my revolver! I nearly wept with relief. I could fire at the wolves without worrying about running out, and I could possibly even take down some larger game. But there was no hammer, so I had to use a flat stone I found outside the front door. My goal was to cover the broken windows and any other holes in the house as best I could. Not just because of the wolves, but winter was making its appearance, and cold air was coming in. It was harsh, something that I hadn't experienced in a long time.

As I finished boarding up and sat down with Toko, I could finally examine my aching, chilled body. My fingertips were all cracked and bleeding. Every movement came with some sharp pain.

I pulled off my shoes. The story was worse on my feet. They, too, were dry and cracked, with hard calluses on the heels. Some of the nails were black or half broken, and a few toes were purple in color. I stretched my poor, abused feet towards the fire. I felt a mixture of pain and relief. After eating the bland stew, I dragged an old couch up to the fire and lay down on it with my backpack as a pillow, and allowed my body to partially relax. Toko stretched out by the fire as well, resting his head on his paws.

At that moment, I did feel some peace. I knew that I had better enjoy it while it lasted.

In the following weeks, the harsh winter began.

Gathering dry wood quickly became a top priority, as the snow started to come down and freezing temperatures were setting in.

The first day it snowed, I watched it in wonder. I had no memories of seeing snow. Toko jumped in the snow and dug holes in it. However, by nightfall that very same day, the temperatures were so low that Toko and I were no longer enamored of the white stuff.

I had to keep the fireplace going the whole day and night. Outside, we could hear the howling of the wolves. The winter would cause them hardships as far as finding food, so they were back again to take a chance on us.

Because of this, the nights became sleepless, and because of the weather, hunting had to be done during the day. It took me days to get just one rabbit and a tiny bird. Even though I took my rifle with me, I never saw any deer or larger game. I had been able to dry some of the wolf meat, and I fortunately had some supplies left from previous hunts and gatherings.

Finally, the wolves chose the time of their attack. It was a morning that felt even colder than the days before. The hills and farmland were covered in deep snow. I heard them howling, and they emerged on the horizon, right at the top of the hill, and began their advance towards the house.

I tied Toko to the thick leg of an old table, as he kept growling in the direction of the howls and adopted a low stance with his front legs spread.

Through an opening in one window, I took my first shot. Blood sprayed over the white snow as I got one of the white wolves in the neck. He stumbled and then fell into the snow, but the rest kept advancing. As long as their leader, the black wolf, went forward, the rest did also.

They circled the house and scratched at the doors and windows. The house was creaking, and glass flew to the floor. I frantically ran from room to room, shooting with my revolver. Once the chambers were empty, I picked up the rifle again.

Suddenly, I heard a banging noise coming from the boarded-up window in the kitchen. My few nails had not been enough, and the center board fell away to the floor. The large head of the black alpha wolf was inside the room, the wicked teeth snapping, and the mouth salivating. He threw himself against the other boards, trying to get at me.

I took aim and shot him in the head, right between the eyes. His body fell outside the house, and all was silent, except for the wind. I slumped to the floor, relieved and exhausted.

I went over to the table and hugged Toko.

CHAPTER TEN
CITY LIFE

We managed to survive the winter in the old farmhouse, and I even discovered some ancient bottles of fruit in the cellar. I boiled the contents, and the apples and peaches were a welcome change from wolf meat. Fortunately, the fruit did not appear to be contaminated.

As the snow began to melt, the earth around us turned into a muddy, slippery mess, but we welcomed the sight with great joy. It was finally warmer, and we could continue our journey.

It was easy to say goodbye to that torn-up farmhouse where we survived the wolves and barely got through the cold winter.

Toko was aging. He often looked weaker, and he moved more slowly than ever before. The journey, on top of all the years in the desert, was taking its toll on him. Yet, he had much pride and dignity and never whined; he was there to serve and to help. I could not have asked for a better and braver companion, a truly dear friend, perhaps even a brother.

We spent days trekking through muddy fields and hills, and then! And then we reached a destination I had greatly wondered about–a city. It was on my map, but I wasn't sure if it still existed or had been completely destroyed. So many cities had been wiped out by the weapons of mass destruction.

We spent one last night still in a rural area, with the city in view. I did not know what to expect. I could see buildings still standing, but I wondered about other humans. Would I find anyone there? Would they be sick like Stella and May? Would they be deformed like the creatures in the forest? Or would they be dead? Skeletal remains?

We approached a broken bridge, uninviting, but the only way I could find over a river into the city itself.

Many buildings, although severely damaged, were still standing. A sense of wonder overtook me as I helped Toko get over certain parts of the bridge, even carrying him at times, which clearly hurt his sense of dignity.

All these thoughts swirled inside my head as we stepped onto the first street of the demolished city on this nice, cool morning.

We began to move cautiously down the street. On each side were grey buildings, all damaged in one way or another. Up ahead were some rusty old cars with broken windows. I saw two large rats emerge from underneath them. They took a look at us and then ran away.

Even if there had been remains of human bodies here, I figured the rats had gotten them. As I walked through this graveyard of human history, I saw hundreds of rodents.

Down a side street, I found some partially intact cafes and restaurants. I approached one and peered into the broken glass door.

I could see a peeling blue counter and round black metal tables, and some ovens for baking in the back. On the right side were metal rows for products, but of course, they were empty. Animals had gotten the food stored there, or some humans who were able to survive for a while. There was no way of knowing anymore.

I had read about couples coming into places like this one. Families too. I tied Toko to one of the black tables and sat down on a black metal chair. I placed both arms on the table and closed my eyes. I tried to remember the details of the magazine articles I'd read, the descriptions. They spoke of the aroma of coffee, a warm black drink that millions loved and enjoyed, one that I myself had never tried. How I wish...

You cannot know what you have never experienced, but imagination helps—at least a little bit.

I opened my eyes and felt the

wetness in them. I was surprised. Through all the horrible things, I held strong, but this had stirred my emotions. The thirst to know, the longing for what was gone.

It was a crucial moment in life when a person realized that there was something they wanted to do, experience, or see very badly, but surely never would. It was a hard pill to swallow.

"Toko, there were days, right here in this spot, when dozens of people smiled, talked, laughed, cried. Thousands of conversations went through this space. Thousands of secrets. Thousands of feelings. This spirit… still somewhat lingers here, although none of those people are alive anymore. Oh… how I wish I could know something like that, just for a moment. Just to know what it feels like. For one little moment, a glimpse, just a tiny taste of it. To have that real experience."

I scratched his head as he watched me with curious but tired eyes. His posture indicated his fatigue.

I went and checked the sturdiness of the door. It was fine. The windows weren't completely broken either, and I was able to move some of the shelves to block the gaps. Then I placed a few round tables against the doors.

"We can rest, Toko; tomorrow we will try to get to the other side of the city, and the ocean won't be so far away anymore."

I lay on the floor and placed my head on the backpack. Toko put his head on my chest. I was more tired than I realized, as we were both asleep before sundown.

I was awakened by Toko's growl in the middle of the night. I rubbed my eyes and sat up next to him. Toko was staring into the darkness in the back section of the cafe and growling; the fur on his ruff stood up. My heartbeat elevated even as I tried to remain calm. Maybe some of those huge rats had gotten in? However, he was staring up higher, towards the ceiling.

There was some light coming in from openings higher up on the walls, which we weren't able to cover. As my eyes got used to the dark, I began to see the silhouette.

It must have flown in…or maybe it was its sleeping spot.

A large bat hung upside down above us. Time to time, it would move its wings and also scratch its head.

Needless to say, neither of us got any more sleep after that, just staring at that bat for several hours, me with the rifle ready. Once the sun began to come up, the thing just flew out like we were not even there, most likely to find a darker place. I knew bats were nocturnal; shouldn't it have been hunting during the night? And since when did bats kill animals or humans? I knew bats ate insects, but I doubted they ate human flesh, unless…

Perhaps it had a mutation, and we were its prey. Possibly, it realized that trying to get us was too risky. Toko had again saved my life.

Shaking off the sense of fear and dread, I moved the tables away from the door, and we walked out into the streets again. We had to make haste and use all the daylight we could to leave the city.

More rats were scurrying around than before. It was unnerving to see so many. People were gone. How were they surviving? Were they also looking to make us their next meal? I could see some moving among the old cars and ruins.

We came up upon a large store covered in faded red paint and with a broken-down door. A sign above it read "Musi." The C was missing. I was surprised the other letters remained. I grasped the doorknob. I had to go in.

"Just this one, and then we will just keep going, Toko."

I had always wondered about music and instruments. The oldest man in the settlement had had a guitar. He often spoke about piano and saxophone, and he said "jazz" was a beautiful thing. Just like drinking coffee in a cafe, it was another one of those things that I just couldn't imagine properly. How could I?

I imagine when a child hears music that speaks to their soul for the first time, they have an incredible experience. Perhaps it moves them on the inside.

I entered the store in the hope of finding some instruments still working. On the floor lay guitars that were either completely broken or had lost their strings. In the back stood a piano, if you could call it that, as it was nearly broken into three parts, largely demolished. If this city had crows or magpies, certainly all the shiny metal bits had been taken by them. There were none of those instruments in sight.

However, something familiar in the back of the store caught my eye. I slowly came up to the device on an old wooden stand. My eyes got big as I finally remembered the name. It was a battery-operated record player, but I'd read that the longest time batteries lasted was 35 years. So, if this place had been abandoned before that, then there was no way. I touched the "on" button. It lit up, and the turntable began to move! There was no record, though. I turned it off in fear of wasting the battery life and began to frantically search the back of the store. I found a stack of records in disintegrating cardboard folders. I carefully slid one out of its sleeve.

"Oh my God, please be okay."

I gingerly placed it on the spindle and turned on the player. I set the arm with the needle on the edge of the vinyl. Hoping for the best, but not entirely sure what to expect.

As I sat down, it began playing. Toko's ears perked up as he watched curiously. I was unprepared for the emotions that gripped me as the woman's voice that filled the room. It was smooth and beautiful. My heart was beating hard as I absorbed every second of it, trying to fill my mind, to keep this in my memory. Was this jazz? She sang soulfully, enchanting my soul. It was one of the best experiences of my life.

Then it stopped. It was as if God had given me this moment just to bless me with this unique experience. And I was deeply grateful.

As we turned to leave, I saw several large vultures standing by the doorway, staring at us. The music must have been a shock to them, too. I raised my rifle and shook it.

"Get away! Away!"

Toko barked as well, and the birds flew up to perch upon the higher parts of the ruined buildings, still watching us.

The next few hours consisted of climbing over cars, ruins, and even an airplane. We found several churches, a theater, and museums. The train station was most fascinating, as there were complete train cars that had not been destroyed. It gave me a small glimpse of a past I was too young to remember before it was gone. I was thankful for it. Growing up in the aftermath of the apocalypse was the only life I could remember. The only life I would ever know.

Finally, we reached the northern part of the city, but were met with a nasty surprise. It was mostly flooded, covered in water. We climbed across partially submerged cars and were able to make it to a massive staircase that rose up into an old hotel. The daylight was fading, and I realized that we would have to spend the night in the hotel, then try to get through the flooded area in the morning. I hoped we could find the next bridge that led out of the city after that.

We ascended a great staircase inside the lobby and were able to find a room that still had a proper door. To my surprise, there was a bed with a mattress on it, completely covered in dust. The room looked fine, but the air was heavy and musty with dust. The window was not broken, and that explained why things had remained more or less intact. The rats had overlooked this room? There had to be a reason why the creatures had stayed away. I cracked the window open to let in some air.

I barricaded the door with a piece of furniture, then I lay on the bed with Toko. He was out almost instantly, as my poor companion was beyond exhausted.

The dust floated up in the air above me. I sneezed and coughed, but lying on the mattress was still far more comfortable than anything I had slept on in the last few months. I felt an odd numbing pain in my feet. I realized that they hadn't had this type of rest in a long time, either. I pulled off my boots and looked at my bloody socks. With some effort, I pulled them off. It was not a pretty sight. My feet were essentially one large callus at this point, cracked with dried blood in the cracks, and my toes were dark and twisted. I allowed them to breathe as I lay back again. Toko moved his head to my chest. I hugged him tightly and fell asleep.

I woke up to a deja vu scene as Toko stood on the bed, growling in a low tone and watching the door. As I sat up and my eyes adjusted to the darkness, I saw that the handle was being moved slightly and heard the creaking of the floor just outside, like multiple feet pacing next to the door. I pulled on my socks and boots and took up my rifle. We spent all night watching that door and listening to the sounds.

When dawn came, the sounds did not stop, and whatever was on the other side of the door was still there, waiting for us. I went over to the door and screamed as loudly as I could. The sounds stopped for a few moments, but then they grew even worse. The door was now slightly shaking, and the handle was moving faster. Toko was barking hysterically. I looked out of the window. There were some ledges and broken balconies. I fully opened the window and pulled on Toko's leash.

I slipped on my backpack and slung the rifle over my shoulder. Then I grabbed the dog with my left arm and stepped out onto the first ledge. The stone cracked a bit but did not collapse.

There was a fire ladder a couple of windows down from us. I carefully stepped over to it, hugging the wall of the hotel as best I could with the dog under one arm. Once I got to the ladder,

I climbed down and set Toko down. We were able to travel along what had been raised walls made to retain soil for landscaping along the front of the hotel, so we could avoid the water for a time.

On the other side of the street, I saw a large rat waddle out onto a ledge. Suddenly, the dirty, dark waters moved, and a tentacle quickly grabbed the rat and pulled it under the water. It had happened almost instantly. I pulled Toko farther away from the water, with my back against the hotel's wall.

"What is this damned place…?"

Why had I been surprised? There were no signs of humans, either alive or dead, in this city for a reason. They all had been eaten, taken, and digested. I looked back at the stairs in front of the hotel. The two choices were clear. Go through the hotel and face whatever had been on the other side of my door, or keep trying to skirt the water.

I pulled Toko back towards the hotel. I reasoned that maybe whatever it was was gone now. If not, I would face it. It had to be better than what was lurking beneath those waters, right? It was better to fight an enemy I could see than one I couldn't. There was only one way to find out. It was do-or-die time again. Turning back wasn't an option.

As we came into the lobby, I stopped and listened. There was complete silence. Not a sound, just a faint whistling of the wind outside the crumbling walls and through the broken windows. Even in an abandoned city, there should be some sound. I had seen plenty of rodents on my way here. What silenced them? I felt the tiny hairs on the back of my neck dance in abject terror as I stepped forward. I made sure to calm myself, slow down my heartbeat and breathing, and to step very slowly, paying close attention to everything around me. Even still, I could feel the tension zinging through my nerves.

Then, as we approached the end of a hallway, I heard something else. I shouldered the rifle and turned to see an enormous spider emerge from a corridor.

I aimed right at its ugly head, filled with eyes. The shot rang out, unnaturally loud in the silent building. The spider shook and then backed out of the corridor and out of sight, leaving some disgusting-smelling ooze behind him. I hoped he was mortally wounded.

"Let's go, hurry."

I sped up the pace, now jogging. I figured the spider would not follow, at least for some time. And I hoped it was alone.

It was a short-lived relief when we came out on the other side of the building. Almost everything was covered in that dark, dirty water. Somewhere underneath it, a horrific creature was searching for us, waiting to have a fresh meal. I nervously swallowed and lightly pulled on Toko, shortening his leash.

"We stay close to the walls, boy, come on."

Despite always trying to stay as far as possible from the water while climbing through the ruins, the distance was never great, as almost everything in this sector was flooded.

In the distance, I saw the largest

ruin of a building yet. It stood on a hill and had most likely been the tallest structure here before the apocalypse. If we could get up that hill, I had a feeling that we'd be out of this flooded sector.

Constantly stopping to observe the water, we kept advancing towards that hill. Poor Toko was hesitant, and I had to carry him over the more treacherous parts, which was exhausting. My feet were numb, and I got used to the constant burning in my knees, but it was still uncomfortable. Sweat was dripping into my eyes from my hair, and I could taste the saltiness of it as it ran into my mustache and beard.

The water did seem to be receding as we finally reached the bottom of that hill of ruins. But as I turned my back to climb up another bit of sidewalk, a swift tentacle emerged from the water and grabbed Toko's back legs, pulling him towards the water. Toko howled in pain, and his eyes were filled with desperation. I held the leash, but I too was sliding towards the water, as I desperately hung onto the dog's leash. I quickly drew the revolver and unloaded all six bullets into the tentacle. The last of the revolver's ammunition I was able to salvage from the farm. The grip loosened, and I pulled Toko away and gathered the shaking dog into my arms. With fear and desperation fueling me with adrenaline, I carried Toko up the hill.

I dropped to my knees once we were far enough. I had lost my revolver, but that was okay. Toko was saved. He looked at me and whimpered.

"Toko, you are safe, I got you, boy."

I hugged him tightly and held him for a long time.

This journey had been very different from what I had envisioned for us, but I still felt that it was worth it. There was certain death if we had stayed in the valley. What had I really expected the world to be? It wasn't a fairy tale. The reality was harsh. Here was the real future of humanity, or perhaps the lack of one.

Despite my terror and our state, I knew we had to keep going before it got dark. I went inside the partially destroyed building and took the stairs up as far as they went. From the top of the ruins, I could see the bridge that led out of the city and towards the old highway.

Which led towards the ocean.

CHAPTER ELEVEN
THE LONG LINE

The highway was still mostly in good shape, although I really had no idea what the good condition of such a road would be. I had never seen one in action, never driven a car, in fact, had never ridden in a car, either. The pavement was cracked, and the paint markings were mostly gone.

Each step upon this hard surface brought a brand new shot of pain. Starting in my poor feet, it went all the way up to my hips and back. I guess I was almost out of gas, just like some of the rusty old abandoned cars on this highway. Toko looked gloomy as well, slowly following behind me. Every hour, I had to sit and rest. My vision was blurry, and I had to close my eyes as well. Toko flopped down and placed his head on my worn-out boots each time and panted heavily.

Then, once I felt I could move on, I'd get up and keep going. That ocean had better be worth it, because it might be the last thing I'd see.

As I passed the old cars, I wondered about the people on that particular day when the bombs and rockets hit, when the powerful waves of fire, radiation, and dust had blown through here. I wondered how many were able to get out of the cars and keep going. For how long, too? Weeks? Months? Years?

How about the children? It must have been so hard for the children, so frightening. I tried to remember myself as a child. Sometimes it came to me in my dreams. How scared was I? The memory was so faint, it was in a fog. I did remember the sadness about my dad, and then my mother and brother as well. This sadness was always just under the surface, forever in my heart. I understood it well because it never left me.

How had these people felt when they'd lost their loved ones? When they'd lost the only ones left for them in this world? I looked at Toko. He was now the only one I had left in my world. The only friend, brother, a true companion. As I watched his tired movements and weakened posture, I wondered if he'd make it to see the ocean.

The days on the highway walk were warm. I was able to kill a deer on the third day. We spent nights inside old cars; however, it was seldom restful. We were always aware of nocturnal sounds coming from the bushes and trees. After all the beasts I'd seen during this journey, it was too hard to ever relax.

"I think I'll be able to rest when I'm dead, Toko. Right?"

I'd laugh and he'd watch me, trying to understand.

On the fourth day, I found an old magazine in one of the cars. It had various images of food and its prices. I had no clue what these prices meant, but surely it had been important to people at that time. I sat next to Toko, pointing at the pages. I was glad that I had been taught how to read in the community. Reading a bit, even if limited, helped me understand some things, and now it helped add a little bit of entertainment to my time on the journey.

"You see that? Ice cream. Think that's good? I've never tasted it. And this? Angus burger? What the hell is Angus? Angus…can't remember. Looks dark in this picture. Cheese on top. I tried cheese a long time ago. I remember it was amazing. You'd love it too. Tastes better than the meat that we cook, I tell you that for sure. And what is this!? Haha, it's so ugly. Sushi? That's rice, but there is a bunch of stuff in it. What is that? Those gooey little balls? And is that fish? You seeing this!?"

The dog gave me a bored, tired look.

"Yeah, I know, ridiculous. That's why the world ended. Eating crap like that was probably not good for anyone.

"But what am I saying? Oh, oh,

look at this, a triple cheeseburger. Triple! Who needs that? Maybe that's for a whole family, right? Not for one person, no way. You'd have to labor all day for that to be normal. How do you even bite into that thing?"

I tried opening my jaw as much as I could. The sides of my face hurt.

"Oh yeah," I continued, "you could probably get injured eating a thing like that. And this? Chicken nuggets? We had some chickens, we had eggs, and we had chicken meat too, but what is a nugget?" I wondered. "I guess they cut up the meat and covered it with something, then they cooked it.

"Sodas, yeah, I read about those too, I tried one a while back, and it was horrible, maybe it was too old to be any good. A cup of 'ramen?' What was that?

I have no clue, it looks like food in a cup, but what is ramen? Hmm, there's no picture to show the inside. There is pasta too. We had pasta supplies at the camp, and some canned pasta as well. Canned corn and peas, stuff like that. It all went pretty fast, though."

I flipped the page.

"Dog food!? Look, buddy, oh my God, that's what the dogs ate, those weird pebbles, you see that? Maybe you're lucky you're with me at the end of the world here. At least I feed you meat, right?"

I tossed the magazine to the side. Our break was over, and we just had to keep on going, despite getting slower and slower with each passing day.

The sun dropped down to hide behind the tall trees again. The night breeze came, and I felt it upon my dry skin and cracked lips. I must have looked like such a madman. I patted Toko on the head.

"You look great compared to me, buddy. Look at you."

That night, I found a bigger car than usual. The seats were wide, and Toko situated himself on the right side and stretched out. I sat behind the wheel and pretended to drive. "Woosh, waash, here I come, going so fast!"

Toko raised his head, and it looked like he was almost shaking it.

"Yeah, buddy, I'm losing it." I pointed at my head. "My mind, I'm losing it."

I leaned back in my seat as the sun fully set and the world was plunged into darkness again.

"Maybe I'll see the ocean soon. The dream ocean. A place where there is no pain, no sadness, no sorrow. A place where there are loving people, and we are all together living without fear. In this place, there are no worries, only love and kindness. People smile there…a lot. And dogs! Ahh…they are everywhere, running together, jumping, and you are a leader among them, Toko."

I looked over at him. The dog was sound asleep, his chest rising up and down steadily.

"Yeah…Maybe that's exactly what you are seeing right now."

I stared into the dark forest in front of the car until my eyelids got too heavy.

In my dream, I saw a city, perhaps it was the same one we had just passed through, except it was no longer in ruins, but rebuilt. People drove cars, ate ice cream, burgers, and even that sushi thing. People danced and they drank a dark drink called coffee. I could see the steam from it in the air, but what did it smell like?

I woke up trying to smell the coffee, yet of course, I could not. Toko was already awake, sitting up in the seat. I opened my backpack to get out some of the deer meat that we had recently gotten. I poured water for the dog after he gobbled down a piece of the meat.

"How much longer to the ocean?" I asked. Toko just looked at me.

I took out the map, and according to it, we weren't far away. I hoped this to be true, since it added some strength to my painful steps.

"Come on, boy. We're almost

there."

It was another long day out on the highway, but monotony was somehow a good thing as, thankfully, I encountered no more dangerous beasts. I knew I should be grateful that fatigue and pain had been our only enemies for the past week.

As I trudged slowly on, I wondered about dreams. Where did they come from? Were dreams literally another world? Another life? If I were to die in my dream, would I stop dreaming? Would that world go dark? Perhaps the world would enter another dream. A dream within a dream. Then, what was reality?

Was the pain I felt the real thing, or was it my feelings, hidden deep down and perhaps revealed inside the dreams?

When we bedded down in yet

another abandoned car for another night, I had an extraordinary dream. I was walking along a street. The road was smooth and perfect, and the white-painted lines were fresh and neat. On each side of the road were beautiful homes with porches. Each had a pretty grass lawn in the front and beautiful, colorful flowers by the windows. I could hear bees buzzing, and I was smiling the whole time. Then, on the right side up ahead, I noticed three people standing in the yard of a house, close together. As I came near them, I realized they were my father, mother, and brother. They all had big smiles on their faces.

I stepped onto the lawn, but my father motioned with his hand for me to stop. "Wait, my boy. It's not your time yet."

I stopped, but I was confused. "I don't understand. I just want to hug you. I have missed you so much!"

My mother smiled and nodded. "We know you miss us, but it's not your time yet. You still have tasks to complete."

I looked at my brother. He smiled and spoke to me. "They're right, bro, be patient, our love is forever, and I will see you again soon."

They started to fade, and I began to fall away from them.

Panic surged through my body. "No! Please! I want to be with you! No! God? God!"

My eyes flew open, and I startled awake. My body was soaked with sweat, and I was breathing hard. This time, I awoke before Toko, and he lifted his head in disappointment, watching me.

The sun had just started to come up, and I could see some of the distant light on the horizon at the bottom of the trees.

I sat in one place, simply watching the trees become illuminated. I kept thinking about my dream. Then I embraced Toko.

"Not yet, my friend, not yet."

And so our trek continued, but I could smell a change in the air, and I could feel the breeze becoming stronger.

CHAPTER TWELVE
THE ILLUMINATED

I was enjoying the change in the air. It felt fresh, more humid, and cooler. I noticed that Toko had his head high and smiling, sniffing at the air. Could it be true? Were we finally nearing our destination?

It was only half an hour later that we heard the exceptional sound for the first time. The rhythmic sound of the waves crashing on the shore and then receding. Then, as we surmounted a hill, we saw it.

I sat down right there and stared in astonishment. We made it. We actually made it. For the first time in a long time, I had real hope. The sea was much bigger than I had imagined. The horizon was just the endless ocean, meeting the sky. I felt small compared with its vastness.

As with all things, we can imagine, but nothing can beat the actual experience. The way the waves just kept rolling in and breaking, then retreating, was mesmerizing. The sound of it was soothing. I felt peace.

Toko sat next to me. The breeze moved his ears a little, and his open mouth looked as though he were laughing.

I petted his head. "Was it worth it, my friend? Can we find a home here now?

"Let's go down to the beach."

As we walked down the hill, the wind picked up, and we saw many white birds circling in the air. I couldn't help but laugh with absolute joy. I took off my boots and pulled the socks off. My poor destroyed feet sank into the soft sand, and it was an indescribable mixture of feeling pleasure and pain. I wanted to run in the sand, but I could just barely drag my feet. Toko was frolicking, jumping up and down. Where had his energy come from!?

We stood in the wet sand at the edge of the water and allowed the waves to lap our feet. At first, it was cool, and the salty water made the fissures in my feet sting, but after a few minutes, it became a soothing sensation.

As we walked along the shore, in the distance, I noticed what looked like a passage going up towards a high cliff. It seemed man-made, as it had stones set along each side. That meant that humans were here, or had been at one point.

I pulled Toko towards it and examined the stones. They were clean and neatly organized in lines. This had to have been done recently. Maintaining the stones would have been ongoing to keep them so pristine.

Curious and fascinated, I followed the path. As I got to the top of the cliff, I saw a medium-sized wooden cabin with a garden of flowers around it. I was about to approach when I heard a deep voice behind me. I turned around to see an old man with a grey beard and hair. He wore a white shirt with black stripes and brown pants. He had no weapons.

"Are you here to rob me?" he asked, calmly.

I quickly shook my head. "Oh, God no. Absolutely not."

He looked us over for a moment,

his eyes coming to rest on my feet for a long moment. "You came from far away, didn't you?"

"Yes, many months of travel."

He gestured toward his home. "Do you want to come in and rest? Eat?"

Grateful tears filled my eyes. "Yes, please, that would be wonderful."

He turned towards the cabin. I was surprised that Toko was calm around a strange male, but maybe the man had very good energy about him.

The cabin was cozy but spacious. There was a wooden table by the window, which was open. I sat in one of the two chairs, and Toko lay at my feet. The man began to stir something in two pots.

"Tea and some potatoes. And you can let your dog loose. It's safe around here. I'm Peter, by the way."

I took off Toko's leash and thanked Peter for his hospitality. "How long have you been living here, Peter?"

He looked at me. "Since I was a little boy. My family is from this region. How about you, where did you live before this?"

"The desert. I always wanted to see the ocean."

Peter continued to stir the pots. "So, is it all that you dreamed of?"

I smiled, for the first time in a very long time. "More. It's perfect. It is more calming and soothing than I ever expected."

"Water and humans, so tightly connected."

"Are you alone here, Peter?"

The old man sighed a little. "Yes, now I am alone, but it used to be a community. At one point, we had as many as fifty people. Most died here. A few young couples left. They said they wanted to try the cities, have babies."

I shuddered involuntarily. "Oh no. The cities…"

"Are they very bad?"

I hesitated. Did I want to relive my experience there? "Beasts, rats, vultures. Horrific creatures. It's just awful. There is no way people can survive long in those conditions."

"That's sad to hear. So, do you plan to stay? There are empty cabins around."

My heart filled with an unspeakable, buoyant joy. I nearly shouted, "That would be incredible. I'd love to live my life here. Whatever is left of it."

Peter smiled slightly. "You never know, you could still have much time.

Maybe one day you'll be the one helping someone else on these shores."

"You think there are a lot of people still alive?"

He cocked his head, thinking for a moment. "I wouldn't say a lot, but enough. Maybe one day there will be a fresh start."

"We won't be seeing it, but it sure would be great to witness."

"On your journey, what stayed with you the most?" He brought bowls of potatoes to the table, along with spoons. Then he turned back to the stove, poured cups of tea, and set them on the table as well, seating himself as I spoke.

"There was a woman and her daughter, both sick." I spooned a piece of potato into my mouth. It was delicious. "I liked the woman. I missed connecting with other people in a strong way like that. I'll never forget her. Also, I will always treasure my dog's resilience and loyalty. He is my true brother, and I love him."

Peter reached down to scratch Toko behind his ears. "Dogs are wonderful creatures. I had one also. He lived until the age of twenty. Small, old fellow."

I continued to chew and swallow the soft, nourishing potatoes. "What happened to the rest of the community? How did they die?"

The man shrugged, shaking his head sadly. "Disease, mostly. Some died in fishing or hunting accidents. As you can see, the disease did not get me. Just like you."

"Do you have any idea why?"

"I suppose some people's genes play

a role, maybe blood type. Who knows?" Peter took a bite of his own potatoes. "We probably will never know, at least until humanity is reborn." He looked out the window, thoughtfully. "One day they'll build cities again, with laboratories, and they'll learn why. They'll write books about it. Maybe they'll even have our skeletons to examine. Doing research on those who did not get sick."

I frowned, thinking. "That's funny to consider, in a way. I don't want to worry about the future anymore."

Peter chuckled. "Worry kills fast. It sucks away at our lives. The more we worry, the less we truly see."

"I figured that much."

Touching my hand, Peter said, "But don't fret. The ocean heals. What you've lost in years, the ocean air will recover."

"But the sadness…"

He looked straight into my eyes, his wise beyond my own. "The sadness, the grief for those you loved, that is part of life, part of us. That is the price we pay for being human. Sorrow and pain are part of our composition."

Leaning toward me and squeezing my hand, Peter said, "Embrace those things. A person who feels nothing no longer lives. He is a walking corpse, no better than a beast."

I nodded. Peter got up and collected the dishes, then gave Toko a bowl. He got some fish with his potato.

"I served your friend a bit of a special treat, but tomorrow I'll be fishing and will get us some too."

"The potatoes were so good!"

The man smiled. "I am glad you

enjoyed them."

"Will you teach me to fish?"

Peter laughed. "Of course. Who will feed exhausted travelers when I'm gone?"

We both laughed, but I also knew the old man was serious. After we washed the dishes, he took us behind the cabin and pointed out several other cabins just down the hill, away from the cliffs and water. He let me choose any that I liked and brought us blankets and even a pillow.

"Tomorrow morning, I will show you something. Rest for now."

I lay down with Toko early. The dog crept close to me, and I let him take up half of the pillow. Because it was the most comfortable position I had been in for a long time, sleep came very quickly.

I did not dream, but when morning came, and Peter knocked on the door, I awoke rested for the first time in years.

The old man wore a large hat and beckoned. "Follow me, my friend. Did you sleep well?"

"Yes! It feels almost abnormal."

"I'll fix you a treat after I show you something."

Toko and I followed Peter. He took us just to the left of the settlement. There, close to another cliff, was a long line of wooden crosses, with a stone at the base of each one. I went closer, dropped to my knees, and as the sun rose higher over the ocean, I could see the carved names. I looked up at Peter, who pointed over the water.

"Each morning they are illuminated by the ocean sun, reminding us about their lives."

I was touched. "That's beautiful, Peter."

"Maybe I'll be one of them someday, yes?"

"One of us won't get to be one of them, I guess."

Peter continued to gaze over the water. "One never knows, my friend. Others might come along." He turned and looked at me rather sternly. "Remember, no more worries about the future."

I watched the illuminated stones for a few more minutes, thinking about the lives they must have led, and then Toko and I followed Peter to his cabin.

As I entered, there was an unfamiliar smell, but one that I liked very much. I looked around and saw an open bag filled with dark seeds standing on the table. I picked up one of them and turned to Peter, who was getting some greens ready that he had just gathered from his garden.

"What's this? I like its smell."

"You mean to say you've never had coffee?!"

I felt my mouth expand into a big smile, and my eyes became large. "No, but I'd love to."

"Sit down, my boy. Relax, I'll make you a proper brew."

As he was heating the coffee on the fire, the aroma filled the cabin, and I couldn't help but grin in anticipation. When it was hot and ready, he poured mine into a clay cup and placed it on the table in front of me. At first, I took my time watching the steam rise. I observed the color, and I smelled it. It was a first-time experience that I had to enjoy. Peter sat across from me with his own cup. Toko lay below us, already chewing on a bone that Peter had given to him.

"It's very hot, so sip slowly," he said, a finger raised in warning.

"Yes, sure."

I brought the cup to my mouth and took a tiny sip. It had a strong, bitter, smoky taste. I felt the roasted flavor all through my mouth, and the warmth filled my body.

"No wonder people loved this drink so much. It makes me think of comfort and safety."

"It's good for many things. And may you still have many great first-time experiences while you live here."

We drank coffee and talked for hours. Later, he began to teach me how to fish. The day went by quickly. The weeks went by even faster.

All was good, except nothing could be like a fairy tale. Life was life.

Six months after coming to the ocean, Toko's heart began to fail. Despite the comfortable new life and lots of fresh fish, the long journey had simply caused him too much damage internally.

His breathing became heavy, he coughed nonstop, and he could barely move.

On one warm morning, I held Toko in my arms for the last time. I watched his chest go up and down. He seemed at peace. He watched me with loving eyes as he took his final breath. Tears rolled down my face, falling upon his. I held him for a long time.

That day, I dug Toko a grave by the

cliffs, next to all the others, and chiseled his name into a rock. The ocean played its soothing tune. As I placed his cross into the ground, I watched the rays of the sun fall upon it.

"You are one of the illuminated now, Toko."

The End.

Alexander Semenyuk (also known as Oleksandr Semenyuk) is a Ukrainian-American author. He was born in Lutsk, Ukraine, in 1986. At 14, he immigrated to the United States. Alexander's favorite genres are sci-fi, horror, and fantasy. Early in life, Alexander was greatly influenced by classic literature and, since childhood, dreamed of becoming a writer.

www.ingramcontent.com/pod-product-compliance
Lightning Source LLC
Chambersburg PA
CBHW020130180626
46810CB00004B/1491